PRINCESS STINKY-TOES

and the

Brave Frog Robert

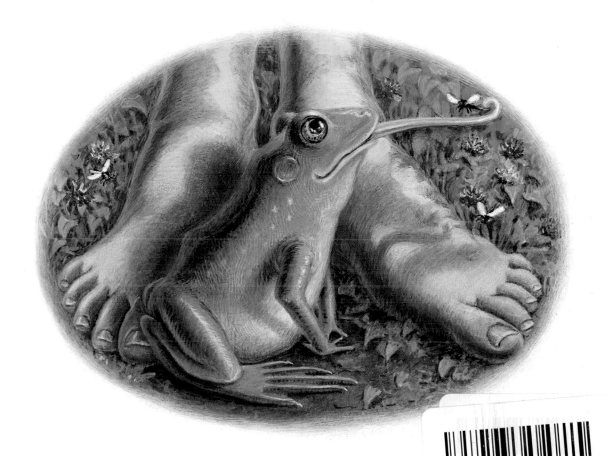

Leslie Elizabeth watts

HarperCollins*Publishers*Ltd

For the Browning girls, the Corley girls,
and the TarBush boys.

And for Princess Emily and the Brave Knight Stefan,
with love.

Produced by Caterpillar Press for
HarperCollins Publishers Ltd
Suite 2900, Hazelton Lanes
55 Avenue Road
Toronto, Ontario M5R 3L2

95 96 97 98 99   First Edition   7 6 5 4 3 2 1

Canadian Cataloguing in Publication Data
Watts, Leslie Elizabeth, 1961-
Princess stinky-toes and the brave frog Robert

ISBN 0-00-224398-9 (bound)
ISBN 0-00-648093-4 (pbk.)
I. Title.

PS8595.A88P65 1995   jC813'.54   C95-931805
PZ7.W38Pr 1995

Hundreds of years ago, in an old stone castle across the sea, a young king and queen fell in love and married. They might have lived happily ever after, but one winter the king became ill, and it seemed certain that he would die.

Then one gray, snowy night, an ancient witch rode a great gust of wind into the castle. "So, your husband is ill," she cackled to the queen. "What would you give if I made him well?"

But when the queen said, "Everything I own," the witch laughed rudely.

"I don't want everything." She plucked a stray straw from her broom and tossed it into the fire where it burned bright blue. "I want your first born child."

"What?" gasped the queen. "Impossible."

"Have it your way," said the witch, straddling her broomstick and aiming it at a high, open window. "It's your choice."

"Wait!" called the queen. "Don't go. I'll agree."

"Done!" said the witch. And, chuckling with glee, she swept into the night.

By morning the king had recovered. The queen was so happy, she could not tell him of her terrible promise.

Late in the spring, their daughter was born. They called her Lunetta, and all the kingdom celebrated. But when she was just a few days old, the witch appeared at the castle and demanded that they hand her over.

This was the first the king had heard of the arrangement, and he tried to put things right. "Please, madam," he said politely. "Take anything you wish from us, but don't take our only child."

"We beg you," said the queen.

The witch grinned hideously. "Very well," she said. "I won't take her this time. After all, my dragon has just eaten."

"You're going to feed her to a dragon?" cried the queen.

"He eats only once in ten years," said the witch. "So you may keep your Lunetta till then. But on the day of her tenth birthday, I will take her to his lair at the top of Mount Blechta, or this kingdom will vanish from the face of the earth." Then she disappeared.

The baby princess grew into a child, and she seemed so merry and sweet that, after awhile, no one could help believing the horrid hag had been just a bad dream.

Then, on Lunetta's ninth birthday, a note was found at the front gate. ONE YEAR TO GO was all it read, and they knew it could only have come from the witch.

Immediately the king proclaimed, "Whoever slays the witch shall receive as much gold as he can carry away." But, although a thousand brave knights traveled the kingdom from one end to the other, the witch was nowhere to be found.

Lunetta could not bear the thought of being eaten. She went to the garden to mull things over, and as she sat at the edge of the pond, a single tear rolled down her cheek and dropped into the water.

No sooner had it fallen than a large spotted frog rose out of the burbling pool. "Whatever is wrong, O Princess?" he inquired.

Lunetta wasted no time in explaining.

"Harrumph," said the frog when she was done. "Just look at me. You'd never know my name was Robert. A long time ago I was a knight, until that same witch cast her spell on me."

The princess didn't hesitate. Very gently, she leaned down and kissed him.

"That's most generous," said the frog, bobbing gracefully. "But if I am to turn back into a knight, I must save someone's life."

"Then I'm afraid you're out of luck," said Lunetta. "No one can save mine."

"Don't be so sure about that," said Frog Robert. "I know that dragon. He used to be a rabbit — then the witch used her magic. He may eat only once every ten years, but he'll have only the sweetest, most tender flesh. I suppose that's why he wants a princess." He lowered his voice. "So, there's only one thing to do. But you can't tell anyone, because the witch is sure to find out."

Lunetta leaned closer, and the wily Frog Robert began to whisper. When he was finished, she said, "But that's disgusting!"

The frog shrugged, making ripples around him. "Ah, well, if you're too much of a princess to stand it, then suit yourself." And he ducked under the water and swam to the bottom.

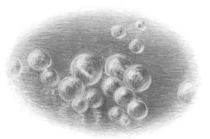

It was almost bedtime when Lunetta arrived home. The king fed her a snack while the queen read a story. But when the Maid of the Bath announced that the princess's tub had been filled, Lunetta shook her head and said, "No."

The king was surprised. "Lunetta," he said. "Bath time."

"No," said the princess.

Now the queen's eyes opened wide. "But, Lunetta, it's bubbles!"

"I don't care."

Her parents looked at one another. At last the queen said, "Very well. You may miss your bath, just this once. But you must have two tomorrow."

However, the following evening when the Maid of the Bath announced that the tub had been filled, again Lunetta said, "No!"

This time the king said, "You must take a bath. I will not have my daughter running about like a street urchin."

"I'm very sad," said the queen. "Very, very sad."

"I'm sorry," said Lunetta, "but I won't change my mind."

The third evening she continued to refuse, and the Maid of the Bath began to complain about wasting water.

"You don't even look like a princess," the queen told Lunetta. "You have a smudge on your cheek, your hair is stringy, and there's sauce on your chin from two days ago."

"But if I'm going to be eaten by a dragon anyway," said her daughter, "who cares if I'm clean or not?"

Her parents had to admit she had a point. So that was that. Other than the new no-bath situation, Lunetta's life continued just as it always had.

You can imagine what happened. Her face was soon filthy, her hair lank and greasy, and her nails filled with dirt. And her feet — oh, my heavens, her feet! To put it bluntly, they stank. In fact, the servants had taken to calling her Princess Stinky-Toes behind her back. (It's likely that the dreadful nickname was started by the Maid of the Bath, who had been sent to the kitchen where she grudgingly peeled potatoes, parsnips, and other root vegetables from dawn till dusk.)

It wasn't long before the Princess's friends stopped coming around, for they were all ashamed to be near someone so smelly. Soon her only companion was Frog Robert, whom she visited every day. He told her many inspiring stories from his days as a knight, and she told him all her secrets.

Six months passed. The royal family attended a masked ball, but the only person who would dance with Lunetta was a duke with a stuffy nose. He whirled her around so fast that one of her glass slippers flew off and landed in the fountain, where it remained for the rest of the evening.

The next day, the duke (much recovered from his cold) brought the newly cleaned slipper to the castle. He was astonished to see Lunetta in daylight, but being well brought up, he said nothing rude. "If you'll put out your foot," he suggested, "I'll replace your missing slipper."

But when Lunetta extended her stinky toes, the unfortunate duke took one sniff and fainted.

"Now will you take a bath?" asked the king.

"No," said Lunetta. "I still won't." And she went to visit Frog Robert.

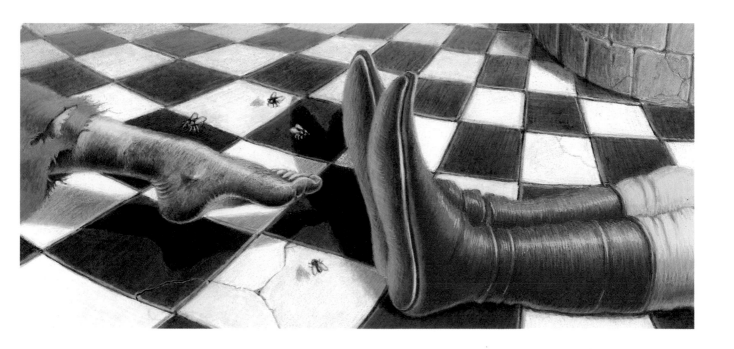

Some time later she was in the west tower, practicing her lute, when a prince rode by. He was so enchanted by the music that he simply had to meet her.

"O Princess, Princess," he called, "let down your hair!"

The music stopped. Lunetta peered out the window. "Who is it?"

"An admirer of fine lutes," replied the prince.

Lunetta shrugged and let her hair hang over the sill. But as the prince stumbled up the grimy tresses, three bats and a cuckoo flew out from under her bangs.

The poor fellow dropped to the ground, leaped upon his steed, and fled on hooves as loud as thunder.

"Will you at least wash your hair?" asked the king.

But her answer was the same: "No, Father, I won't."

Several more months passed. By now the princess spent most of her time in the highest tower. Her parents visited each day, as long as the windows were open and there was a good, stiff breeze. But she had to eat alone. The Maid of Root Vegetables would leave the food tray by the door and run.

On the last day of her tenth year, Lunetta sat down by the pool. "Frog Robert!" she called. "Are you there?"

A moment later, he was at her side.

"Tomorrow," said Lunetta, "the witch will take me to the top of Mount Blechta, and her dragon will eat me." And she began to cry.

"Fear not," said Frog Robert. "You have done well to take my advice."

"I have no friends," wept the princess. "My hair is grungy, my skin is bad, and my feet stink."

"It's true you are unusual," admitted the frog, "but your oddness may prove to be a good thing in the end. And I," he said, drawing himself up proudly, "am your friend."

"That's very kind of you," said Lunetta, "but I'm still frightened."

"Then put me in your pocket," said Frog Robert, "and I will give you courage."

So when the moon rose over the garden, Princess Lunetta returned to her tower with the brave Frog Robert wrapped in a wet hanky to keep him moist.

Lunetta could not eat, but she was glad to pick flies and spiders out of her hair for her companion. After the king and queen had kissed her good night, Frog Robert hopped onto the pillow beside her head and began to chuggarumph a beautiful lullaby. But the princess was sleepless with fear. At midnight she got up and looked in the mirror.

"I don't look anything like myself," she thought. "Maybe I should have a quick wash so my parents can see how I really look before I'm eaten."

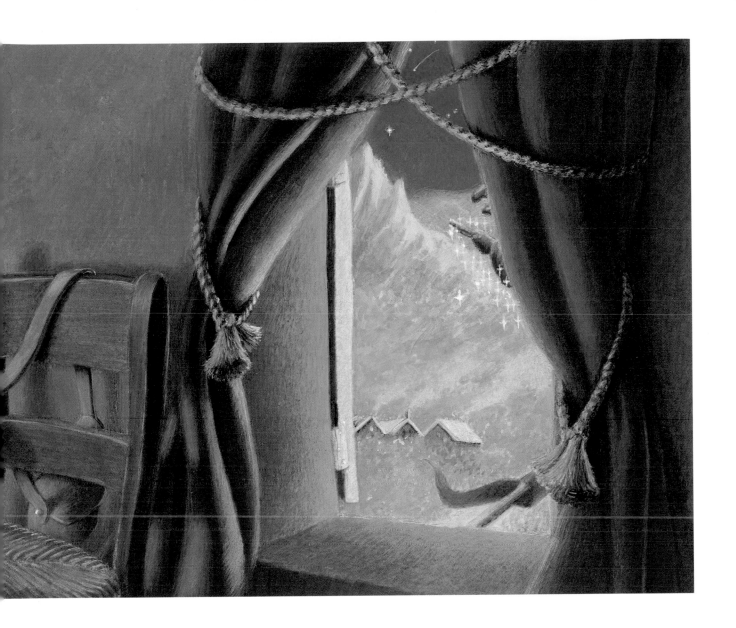

As if he could read her mind, Frog Robert said, "No! Promise me you won't do it!"

"All right, dear Frog," said Lunetta.

As she picked him up tenderly, they heard the witch's cackle, carried towards them by the wind.

"Quickly," whispered the frog. "Blow out the candle so she cannot see how you look."

Lunetta had barely enough time to slip the frog into her pocket before the witch blasted through the window. "But you're so early," said the princess. "I haven't said goodbye to my parents."

"Tough toadstools," screeched the witch. "Now come along! It will soon be dawn, and my dragon is hungry."

Then she dragged Lunetta onto her broom and they flew out the window. The princess might have cried, but when she put her hand in her pocket, she could feel the frog's heart beating steadily under his cool skin, and it made her brave.

At last the witch set her broom down on the rocky mountainside. "We must walk from here," she said.

The woods were dark and the path treacherous. Several times the princess stumbled.

"Hurry, hurry," urged the witch. "I can hear his stomach rumble."

Suddenly there was a dreadful roar above them — so loud that the ground trembled and the trees swayed.

"Where is my breakfast?" hissed the dragon. "I'm simply ravenous."

"Over here!" shrieked the witch. "Come and get it!"

The dragon began to approach, but just as he
reached Lunetta, the sun rose over the top of
Mount Blechta, and the shadows fell away from
the princess. The dragon stopped in his tracks.
A great raft of steam rose from his nostrils, and he
narrowed his yellow eyes. "What," he asked, "is this filthy,
wretched thing?"

"A princess, you fool!" cried the witch. "Your favorite food!"

The dragon slithered closer. He sniffed the air, and the two
points of his tongue darted out between his teeth. Then he
began to cough.

"What are you waiting for?" screamed the repulsive hag.
"Eat her!"

The dragon opened his huge mouth, and Lunetta thought
she was done for. But he roared again, even more loudly
than before.

"I cannot believe this crusty, putrid creature is a princess,"
he told the witch. "I think you're trying to trick me. She's far more
disgusting than you. But I'm still very, VERY hungry." He put his
head next to hers. "What do you think I should do?"

"Eat her anyway?" she guessed.

"Blech!" said the dragon. "I'd rather eat you."
And before the old hag could say lizards' gizzards,
he swallowed her whole.

Immediately, the scaly, hissing creature disappeared, and in its place sat a plump, white rabbit, burping softly and wriggling its nose. It bowed deeply, said, "Thank you, madam," to the astonished princess, and lolloped into the trees.

Almost at once, Frog Robert grew so large and heavy that the pocket tore right off Lunetta's tattered skirt.

"Oh!" she gasped. "You're human!"

And so he was. The brave frog had turned into Sir Robert, a fine-looking knight with a big grin. "I guess I must have broken the spell," he said modestly.

Princess Lunetta looked down. "And now that you're a person," she said sadly, "I suppose you'll be too ashamed to have me for a friend."

"On the contrary," said the knight. "I admire your ability to be different under trying circumstances. Then he took Lunetta by the arm, and they returned to the castle, where there was a huge celebration.

In the midst of the ruckus, the princess sneaked away to the kitchen, where the Maid of Root Vegetables was hard at work on a sack of potatoes.

"I'm sorry to bother you," said Lunetta, "but I've had quite a year. If you have a moment, would you mind pouring me a bath?"

"Delighted," said the maid, tossing down her paring knife. And she never peeled another vegetable as long as she lived.